SPORTS GREAT CHRIS WEBBER

—Sports Great Books—

BASEBALL

Sports Great Jim Abbott
0-89490-395-0/ Savage

Sports Great Bobby Bonilla
0-89490-417-5/ Knapp

Sports Great Orel Hershiser
0-89490-389-6/ Knapp

Sports Great Bo Jackson
0-89490-281-4/ Knapp

Sports Great Greg Maddux
0-89490-873-1/ Thornley

Sports Great Kirby Puckett
0-89490-392-6/ Aaseng

Sports Great Cal Ripken, Jr.
0-89490-387-X/ Macnow

Sports Great Nolan Ryan
0-89490-394-2/ Lace

Sports Great Darryl Strawberry
0-89490-291-1/ Torres & Sullivan

BASKETBALL

Sports Great Charles Barkley
(Revised)
0-7660-1004-X/ Macnow

Sports Great Larry Bird
0-89490-368-3/ Kavanagh

Sports Great Muggsy Bogues
0-89490-876-6/ Rekela

Sports Great Patrick Ewing
0-89490-369-1/ Kavanagh

Sports Great Anfernee Hardaway
0-89490-758-1/ Rekela

Sports Great Juwan Howard
0-7660-1065-1/ Savage

Sports Great Magic Johnson
(Revised and Expanded)
0-89490-348-9/ Haskins

Sports Great Michael Jordan
(Revised)
0-89490-978-9/ Aaseng

Sports Great Jason Kidd
0-7660-1001-5/ Torres

Sports Great Karl Malone
0-89490-599-6/ Savage

Sports Great Reggie Miller
0-89490-874-X/ Thornley

Sports Great Alonzo Mourning
0-89490-875-8/ Fortunato

Sports Great Hakeem Olajuwon
0-89490-372-1/ Knapp

Sports Great Shaquille O'Neal
(Revised)
0-7660-1003-1/ Sullivan

Sports Great Scottie Pippen
0-89490-755-7/ Bjarkman

Sports Great Mitch Richmond
0-7660-1070-8/ Grody

Sports Great David Robinson
(Revised)
0-7660-1077-5/ Aaseng

Sports Great Dennis Rodman
0-89490-759-X/ Thornley

Sports Great John Stockton
0-89490-598-8/ Aaseng

Sports Great Isiah Thomas
0-89490-374-8/ Knapp

Sports Great Chris Webber
0-7660-1069-4/ Macnow

Sports Great Dominique Wilkins
0-89490-754-9/ Bjarkman

FOOTBALL

Sports Great Troy Aikman
0-89490-593-7/ Macnow

Sports Great Jerome Bettis
0-89490-872-3/ Majewski

Sports Great John Elway
0-89490-282-2/ Fox

Sports Great Brett Favre
0-7660-1000-7/ Savage

Sports Great Jim Kelly
0-89490-670-4/ Harrington

Sports Great Joe Montana
0-89490-371-3/ Kavanagh

Sports Great Jerry Rice
0-89490-419-1/ Dickey

Sports Great Barry Sanders
(Revised)
0-7660-1067-8/ Knapp

Sports Great Deion Sanders
0-7660-1068-6/ Macnow

Sports Great Emmitt Smith
0-7660-1002-3/ Grabowski

Sports Great Herschel Walker
0-89490-207-5/ Benagh

OTHER

Sports Great Michael Chang
0-7660-1223-9/ Ditchfield

Sports Great Oscar De La Hoya
0-7660-1066-X/ Torres

Sports Great Wayne Gretzky
0-89490-757-3/ Rappoport

Sports Great Mario Lemieux
0-89490-596-1/ Knapp

Sports Great Eric Lindros
0-89490-871-5/ Rappoport

Sports Great Steffi Graf
0-89490-597-X/ Knapp

Sports Great Pete Sampras
0-89490-756-5/ Sherrow

SPORTS GREAT CHRIS WEBBER

Glen Macnow

St. Lawrence School
44429 Utica Rd.
Utica MI 48087

—Sports Great Books—

Enslow Publishers, Inc.
40 Industrial Road   PO Box 38
Box 398   Aldershot
Berkeley Heights, NJ 07922   Hants GU12 6BP
USA   UK
http://www.enslow.com

*To Lois Stone, who could write volumes about hard work,
overcoming adversity, and the love of family*

Copyright © 1999 by Enslow Publishers, Inc.

All rights reserved.

No part of this book may be reproduced by any means without the written permission of the publisher.

Library of Congress Cataloging-in-Publication Data

Macnow, Glen.
   Sports great Chris Webber / Glen Macnow.
     p. cm. — (Sports great books)
   Includes index.
   Summary: Examines the life and basketball career of Chris Webber, discussing his successes at the University of Michigan and in the National Basketball Association.
   ISBN 0-7660-1069-4
   1. Webber, Chris, 1973– —Juvenile literature. 2. Basketball players—United States—Biography—Juvenile literature. [1. Webber, Chris, 1973– . 2. Basketball players. 3. Afro-Americans—Biography.] I. Title. II. Series.
GV884.W36M33   1999
796.323'092—dc21
[B]   98-35039
                             CIP
                             AC

Printed in the United States of America

10 9 8 7 6 5 4 3 2 1

To Our Readers:
All Internet addresses in this book were active and appropriate when we went to press. Any comments or suggestions can be sent by e-mail to Comments@enslow.com or to the address on the back cover.

Illustration Credits: Andrew D. Bernstein/NBA Photos, pp. 36, 39, 41; Andy Hayt/NBA Photos, p. 18; Barry Gossage/NBA Photos, pp. 23, 56; Bill Baptist/NBA Photos, p. 53; Frank McGrath/NBA Photos, p. 14; Jeff Reinking/NBA Photos, p. 58; Layne Murdoch/NBA Photos, p. 59; Lou Capozzola/NBA Photos, p. 32; Mitchell Layton/NBA Photos, p. 27; Nathaniel S. Butler/NBA Photos, pp. 10, 46; Sam Forencich/NBA Photos, pp. 12, 21, 29; Scott Cunningham/NBA Photos, pp. 44, 49.

Cover Illustration: Andy Hayt/NBA Photos.

Contents

Chapter 1 7

Chapter 2 16

Chapter 3 25

Chapter 4 34

Chapter 5 42

Chapter 6 51

   Career Statistics 61

   Where to Write 62

   Index 63

Chapter 1

Most great athletes are remembered for their achievements: a world championship, scoring title, Most Valuable Player award. A star athlete's success is usually what puts him in the spotlight.

But Chris Webber is different. Sure, Webber is a basketball star. He has been a great player at the high school, college, and pro levels. He has earned awards and honors and has produced tremendous highlights.

More than anything else, however, Chris Webber is remembered for his one great moment of failure. Or maybe it is better to put it this way—he is remembered for the classy way in which he handled that failure. You can tell a lot about a man by how gracefully he deals with defeat.

The moment came in April 1993. Webber, then twenty years old, was the power forward for the University of Michigan Wolverines. What a team this was. The Wolverines' lineup boasted five sophomores—the Fab Five, as they were known. They were the best recruiting class in the history of college basketball. The Fab Five were a loud and boastful group. They wore baggy shorts down to their knees and high-fived their way to win after win. At the end of the regular season, they had won 26 games and lost just 4. Webber, who led the team in scoring and rebounding, was the biggest star.

Now the Wolverines were in the National Collegiate Athletic Association (NCAA) championship game against the Tar Heels of the University of North Carolina. The game was close throughout, and Webber was brilliant. He contributed 23 points and 11 rebounds.

But none of that would be remembered at the final buzzer. All that would be recalled—for years to come—was Webber's big goof.

With less than a minute to go, Michigan trailed by two points. Wolverines head coach Steve Fisher talked to his team. He drew up a last-ditch strategy to win the game. As the huddle broke, Fisher reminded his players that they had no timeouts left. Unfortunately, Webber did not hear his coach's last words—or did not understand them.

The game resumed. Webber grabbed a missed foul shot and began dribbling up the court. Sixteen seconds were left. Webber could tie the game with a two-point basket. A three-pointer could win it.

Two Tar Heels dogged Webber as he moved upcourt. He felt the pressure. Now there were thirteen seconds left. Now there were twelve. With eleven seconds remaining, and two opponents blocking his way, Chris Webber choked. He covered up and brought his hands together in a T, looking to the referee for a timeout.

Immediately, both benches exploded—North Carolina's in joy, Michigan's in agony. By signaling a timeout when his team had none left, Webber had committed a technical foul. Under the rules, that meant two foul shots for the Tar Heels. Also, it meant that North Carolina would get the ball back after the foul shots. Suddenly, Michigan's chances for a national title were gone.

"We had our hands on the trophy," Webber said afterward. "But we had butterfingers. And I was the butter."

Carolina went on to win the game. As he walked off the court in front of sixty thousand fans at the Superdome in New Orleans, and a national TV audience of millions, Webber hung his head in shame.

But a funny thing happened. Instead of being despised as a goat, Webber became a popular person. Partly, that happened because people understood the pain a great player was going through. "No one feels worse than Chris," Coach Fisher said. "We're not here in this game if it's not for Chris."

Maybe more so, fans appreciated the classy way Webber handled the moment. Instead of running and hiding, he faced up to failure. After the game, he answered all of the reporters' questions. He showered, dressed, and left the locker room. He walked through a hallway, head down. He stopped to sign a few autographs for kids. Then Webber saw his father. He began to cry in his father's arms.

For days afterward, Webber took every question. He owned up to his mistake and said he had learned much from it. "You not only find out who your friends are when something like this happens," he said. "You find out you have friends you didn't even know about."

Since then, Chris Webber has gone on to greater things. Just months after the 1993 NCAA Championship Game, he was the first player chosen in the National Basketball Association (NBA) draft. He wound up with the Golden State Warriors, who changed his position from power forward to center. Webber was the youngest player among more than three hundred in the NBA that year, but his play did not show it. In 1993–94, he became the first rookie in NBA history to get more than 1,000

Even star athletes make mistakes in big games. Although Chris Webber felt terrible after his timeout cost Michigan a chance to win the game, he learned from his error.

points, 500 rebounds, 250 assists, 150 blocks, and 7. season's end he was voted NBA Rookie of the Year.

"He has the mental and physical capacities to be player," said Warriors coach Don Nelson." And the d there. He just has to be the best. It's driven in him. I on't know where it came from, but I love it. He can't miss."

In recent years, Webber has come to be regarded as one of the NBA's most dangerous players. He is a big man who can dribble among the speedsters. He can crash the boards with the nastiest of giants. He is equally dangerous shooting from the outside or driving to the hoop.

"Ten years from now, I'd like to be regarded in the same breath as Larry Bird, Magic Johnson, and Michael Jordan," Webber once said. "I don't know if I'll ever get there, but I'm going to try."

While looking toward the future, Webber has not forgotten his past. And always, he has remembered the big mistake against North Carolina—and how friends and family helped him pull through it. On the Sunday after the loss, for example, Webber and his family met at his grandmother's house for dinner. When it came time for a premeal prayer, Webber's mother formed a T with her hands and said, "Okay, timeout." The whole family used the word again and again that day, until it became less painful.

"My family has never let me feel too sorry for myself," Webber said.

Mayce Edward Christopher Webber III was born on March 1, 1973, in Detroit, Michigan. From the start, he was called Chris, to avoid any confusion with his father. Mayce Webber, Jr., Chris's dad, worked at a Cadillac plant. He often worked double shifts in order to feed and clothe his family. Chris's mom, Doris, was a high school teacher who sewed her children's clothes to save money. The family was not poor, but

Webber left school to play in the NBA after the 1992–93 college season. At the end of the 1993–94 season, he was voted NBA Rookie of the Year.

they were not rich either. They lived in a decent house in a middle-class neighborhood.

Chris was the eldest of five children—four boys and a girl. From a young age, he took care of the others, making them lunch and changing their diapers. Chris loved being part of a close-knit family. He didn't mind when other kids teased the Webbers, calling them "The Brady Bunch," or "The Waltons." Both nicknames came from popular television shows featuring loving families.

Chris's parents were loving but strict. They made sure that the five kids took their schooling seriously. Every night, the television would go off for an hour of "quiet time," in which the children could read or think. There was no talking and no playing allowed during the hour.

"When I'd get home from school, I'd want to go outside and play," Webber recalled. "My street must have had fifty kids on it, so everybody would be in the street playing. But I couldn't play until I cleaned up. And then my mom would make us read for an hour. I didn't like it then. But now I'm glad she made me do it."

From the start, this future hoops star was very large. The doctor who delivered him predicted that Chris would grow to be seven feet tall. (Chris eventually made it to six feet ten inches.) As a child, he was a big eater and a quick learner. He was walking by the time he was ten months old. At a little over one year, he was able to play catch. By kindergarten, he was a head taller than the other children.

Because he was so tall, people pushed Chris to play basketball. He and his brothers used to take on their dad in their driveway, pretending they were NBA stars Magic Johnson or Bernard King. The idea of playing organized basketball, however, scared Chris. He was a bit clumsy as a child. He did not have much self-confidence.

Posting up against a smaller opponent, Webber has a clear shot at the basket. When Webber was born, the doctor said he would grow to be seven feet tall.

But Mayce Webber insisted that his son sign up for a summer league before he entered sixth grade. Chris—who was nearly six feet tall by then—showed up for the first game in a goofy Hawaiian shirt that drew laughs from the other boys. He was shy and sensitive. He apologized if he fouled another player. He sulked when the other boys teased him.

His chief tormentor that day was a beanpole of a kid named Jalen Rose. Years later, they would become best friends and teammates. But on this day, Jalen just walked up to Chris and said, "You've got the sorriest game I've ever seen." Chris nearly broke down and cried.

After two practices, Chris went home and told his parents he was quitting basketball. His father would not hear of it. "A man doesn't run away from difficult situations," Mayce Webber told his boy. "He stands firm and conquers them."

So Chris went back. He didn't know whether he would ever become good at the sport, but he decided to give it his best try. He did not want to be teased anymore. And he did not want to disappoint his father.

It turned out to be one of the smartest moves he ever made.

Chapter 2

Young Chris Webber was extremely clumsy when he first started playing basketball. Still, there was no doubt that this giant of a boy had talent inside him. The first person to spot it was a coach named Curtis Hervey.

Hervey coached Chris in a summer league when Chris was just eleven years old. While others laughed at the gangly boy who could not dribble the ball without hitting his own feet, Coach Hervey saw a future star in the making. He spent hours that summer teaching Chris the basic moves. He made sure that Chris was surrounded by good teammates—like future college teammate Jalen Rose—so that Chris could learn from them. And he decided to toughen Chris up. During practices, he ordered other players to tease Chris.

"Get on this kid," Coach Hervey told the others. "Hit him. Talk about his mama, whatever. Don't let up."

The strategy might seem mean, but it was not intended to be. It was a plan to get the shy and gentle child to play as if he were a little angry. At first, Chris sulked. But his father and his coach told him to fight back—by playing better ball. Soon he learned to play aggressive basketball. In making Chris tougher, Coach Hervey made him a better player.

By the time Chris was thirteen, he was starring for an Amateur Athletic Union (AAU) team that was touring the country. His club was called the Super Friends. Hervey coached the team, which also included Jalen Rose and eight other Detroit teenagers. They played in tournaments around the United States. For two years, Chris was the Most Valuable Player of the AAU Junior Olympic Games. Suddenly, the once-shy kid was being interviewed on television.

Chris was just an eighth grader when college coaches began inviting him to visit their schools. To the Webber family, that seemed crazy. After all, he had not even chosen a high school yet.

Most teens attend the high school in their neighborhood. But for some athletic stars—especially in basketball-crazy states such as Michigan—the process is not that simple. Those kids are recruited by public and private high schools. The schools are hoping that the young stars will bring glory and attention to their institutions.

Chris was getting offers from many high schools. Most people figured he would go to one of the big Detroit schools that developed other NBA stars like Derrick Coleman and Kevin Willis. But against everyone's wishes—except his parents'—Chris enrolled in Detroit Country Day School, a tiny private suburban school.

To many people, this seemed a curious choice. First of all, it cost thousands of dollars for tuition. Chris's parents were not poor, but they were far from rich. Paying for school would be a struggle. Also, Country Day was great for academics, but not for sports. Clearly, Chris was better than anyone else who would play basketball there. But education came first, his parents insisted. They wanted Chris to learn in school. If he

Making an explosive move to the basket, Webber dunks over Vancouver's Mike Bibby. Webber can thank his former AAU coach, Curtis Hervey, for being one of the people who taught him to be an aggressive player.

played basketball also, that was fine. But learning would come first.

At first, Chris did not like the school at all. There were very few city kids like himself, and there were almost no other African-American students. Most of his classmates were wealthy. That made him self-conscious.

"We had to wear a suit to school every day. I didn't even have a suit," he recalled. "I saw kids getting new cars on their sixteenth birthday. Then I would go home and eat beans for a week."

Still, he worked hard to keep his grades up. And when it came to basketball, he did not have to take a backseat to anyone. Even as a freshman, Chris was a star in the suburban private school league. None of his teammates on the Country Day Yellow Jackets were as talented as Rose and his other old friends. None of his opponents could stop him.

As a freshman, Chris was voted to an all-state team by writers and broadcasters from around Michigan. As a sophomore, he averaged 25 points, 12 rebounds, and 6 blocked shots a game. That season, the Yellow Jackets beat Ishpeming High School to win the state's Class C championship.

By the time he was a junior, Chris stood six-feet eight-inches tall. Country Day High School moved up to a tougher division, but it still provided little competition. The Yellow Jackets won the state Class B title, beating Saginaw's Buena Vista, the previous year's champion. Chris scored 30 points in the title game.

In his final year of high school, Chris was a celebrity. More than one hundred college coaches tried to lure him to attend their schools. His old sneakers and knee pads became collectors' items among Yellow Jackets fans, who expected him to grow up to become an NBA All-Star. Detroit Country Day again won the state title—the third year in a row. And Chris was named *Parade* magazine's National High School Player of the Year. His parents had been proven right. He had spent four years learning in a tough academic school, and he had lost nothing in basketball.

Now, everyone wondered about where he would go to college. A talent as good as this could lead a college to a national title. But Chris's priorities meant that the school would also have to be a place where he could learn.

On March 23, 1991, Chris and his Yellow Jackets teammates celebrated their third straight state championship. Then Chris announced his plans. He would attend the University of Michigan in nearby Ann Arbor. The school has a great athletic tradition. Equally important, it is a topflight academic university.

"I don't want to be a dumb athlete," Chris said that night. "Today in America, and especially being black, you need everything you can get. I need a good education."

There were a few other things that impressed him about Michigan. A month earlier, he had attended a game at the university's Crisler Arena. When Wolverines fans spotted him in the stands, they began cheering, which really made him feel wanted.

Also, Chris was not alone. His neighborhood buddy, Jalen Rose, had signed up to attend Michigan. The old AAU teammates would be reunited. In fact, they would be college roommates.

When Webber and Rose showed up in Ann Arbor in 1991, they learned they were not the only freshman stars on the team. Coach Steve Fisher had recruited three others—Juwan Howard, Jimmy King, and Ray Jackson. Before they played a game, the five were being touted as the greatest recruiting class in college basketball history. They even earned a nickname—the Fab Five.

The Fab Five were different from any other group who had

Double-teamed, Webber tries to get the shot off. Chris Webber is use to drawing a crowd. When he was in high school, over one hundred college basketball coaches tried to persuade him to attend their schools.

come before them. Even as first-year players, they were loud and confident. Their fans called them fun and exciting. Critics called them boastful and disrespectful. They celebrated baskets and pointed fingers and talked trash to opponents. Even their uniforms were different. They wore baggy, knee-length shorts. Webber actually started the look to cover a scar on his thigh, but it caught on as a fashion trend that stayed popular for years.

Love them or hate them, there was no denying this group's talent. In their first game, in Detroit's Cobo Hall, the Wolverines rolled over the University of Detroit Mercy by a score of 100–74. Webber finished with 19 points and 17 rebounds. On the downside, he also had 7 turnovers and fouled out.

Michigan plays in the Big Ten Conference, one of the best in college basketball. It is rare for a freshman to win a starting spot on a Big Ten team. It is more unusual for two to start. But by the middle of the 1991–92 season, all five Michigan freshmen were in Coach Fisher's starting lineup, something previously unheard-of. Webber was their leader on the floor, and what success he had!

Webber became the first freshman ever to lead the Big Ten in rebounding, with 9.8 per game. He also led the conference in steals. He averaged 15.5 points per game. By contrast, Michael Jordan averaged 13.5 points when he was a freshman at the University of North Carolina, and Charles Barkley averaged 12.7 as a freshman at Auburn University.

The Wolverines finished the regular season with 20 wins and just 8 losses. They were ranked the fourteenth best college team in the country. Still, most experts did not think they would go far in the 1992 National Collegiate Athletic Association (NCAA) Tournament, which features sixty-four teams going for the national title. They were so young and inexperienced. How would they fare against older, more tested teams?

To win the NCAA Tournament, a team must win six

Chris Webber and Juwan Howard played together first as part of the University of Michigan Wolverines' "Fab Five," and later for the Washington Bullets (renamed Wizards) in the NBA.

games in a row. Each round gets a bit tougher. Michigan slipped by Temple University, 73–66. Then the Wolverines easily beat East Tennessee State. Webber hit on twelve of fifteen shots in that game. Next, the Wolverines beat the University of Oklahoma, which made them one of eight teams left alive in the field.

This is where most experts expected the Fab Five's fun ride to end. They next had to face Ohio State University, a Big Ten opponent that had already beaten them twice. Ohio State's big center, Chris Jent, had stifled Webber the first two times they met.

But this game was different. Seconds before it started, a few of the Wolverines appeared a bit nervous on the court. So Webber walked up to Rose and planted a kiss on his teammate's cheek. It cracked the team up and made all the players a bit looser.

Early in the first half, Webber took a pass from Howard and rose up for a dunk. Jent leaped too, trying to block the way. Webber somehow hung in the air while Jent went up and then down again. Webber crashed the ball through the hoop—rattling the backboard and sending a message.

A few minutes later, Jent tried to return the favor. But when the Ohio State center leaped to try a slam dunk, Webber came from the side and smacked the ball out of Jent's hands. "Not tonight," Webber shouted at Jent. "Tonight, we own the ball."

The game went into overtime before Michigan took away a 75–71 win. Suddenly, this squad of freshman upstarts was in the running for the national title. The Fab Five was going to the Final Four.

Chapter 3

Chris Webber had played in big games in his young life. For three straight years, he had led his high school team to the Michigan state championship. But college was different. This was the big time. And now, the same month he turned nineteen years old, Webber was leading the Michigan Wolverines into the NCAA Final Four.

Shortly before the tournament, the team got to meet former heavyweight champion Muhammad Ali. The great boxer was known in his day for his brashness and high energy—just like the Fab Five. The young basketball players took a liking to Ali. He told them to believe in themselves. If they did, he said, they could win it all—just as he had. From that point on, Webber and his teammates began using one of Ali's old slogans. "We're gonna shock the world," they boasted.

With four teams left in the running for the 1992 national title, Michigan faced the University of Cincinnati Bearcats. It was not much of a game. The Wolverines dominated from the start. Michigan won, 87–72. Webber led the way with 21 points.

Now the five freshman were suddenly playing for the

national title. No one had expected this going into the tournament. People around the country began following this loud group of trash-talking youngsters. Basketball fans seemed to either love or hate the team. Nobody was in the middle.

The Wolverines faced the Duke University Blue Devils for the championship. The young Fab Five had to deal with Duke coach Mike Krzyzewski's experienced players. Duke had won the NCAA title a year earlier and had been runner-up the year before that. For Webber, facing Duke meant a personal matchup with star forward Christian Laettner, a smart and tough senior forward. Certainly, Michigan had its work cut out.

Before sixty thousand fans in person and millions watching on television, the young Wolverines got off to a great start. A few minutes into the game, Webber brought the crowd to its feet by dunking over Laettner. Moments later, Webber tossed a behind-the-back pass to Michigan substitute Rob Pelinka for an open jump shot. At halftime, the Wolverines led, 31–30. Maybe they could follow Ali's advice and shock the world.

But in the second half, Duke's experience came through. The Blue Devils tightened up on defense and began to find the open man on offense. In the end, Duke thrashed the Fab Five with a score of 71–51. Webber ran to the locker room so that TV cameras would not catch him crying.

"I wanted to fight back the tears," he said. "I really tried. But I'm human. I hurt. I couldn't stop myself. I didn't want to wait for something I've been dreaming about since I was six years old in the backyard, playing one-on-one with my father. The dream was right there."

Sure he was disappointed. But he was just nineteen years old. There would be other chances.

That summer, Webber received a high honor. He was among a handful of college players invited to play on a

Chris Webber elevates for a lay-up against Doug West (number five) and Cherokee Parks of the Minnesota Timberwolves. Parks was a member of Duke's 1992 NCAA Championship team that beat Webber's Michigan Wolverines.

basketball developmental squad recruited to scrimmage against the United States Olympic team. Still a teenager, he was on the court, facing his heroes, like Michael Jordan, Magic Johnson, Larry Bird, and Clyde Drexler. To Webber's delight, he held his own against those great stars. It was a real confidence builder.

As the 1992–93 season began, the Fab Five had more confidence. Though they were only sophomores, they were looking to win the national title. They were also the most exciting team in the country. They were young and a bit wild. They thrilled fans with fancy dunks and no-look passes. They celebrated and woofed and did not try to hide their happiness. In addition to baggy shorts, they now all wore black socks, and they shaved their heads.

One day, Webber was asked if the Fab Five's style might seem immature for college players. "Earlier this season we were thinking, 'We're older now, we're sophomores, so let's be serious and businesslike on the court,'" he said. "But we're happier when we are just ourselves, not holding our emotions back."

Still, their behavior bothered some. After beating rival Michigan State University, Webber and teammate Ray Jackson jumped on the scorer's table and performed a victory dance. And in a game against Indiana, Webber followed a slam dunk by pointing his finger right under the nose of Hoosier coach Bobby Knight. Being brash was one thing. Being rude and unsportsmanlike was another.

Webber did not understand why anyone would be offended. "I just wink at my players and make faces at the crowd," he said. "I'm a very emotional person. I just have to have freedom to express myself on the court after a good play because it keeps me going."

Certainly, Webber backed up his talk. As a sophomore, he

Chris Webber is a very emotional player who likes to express himself on the court.

led the team in most important categories. He averaged 19.2 points per game, along with 10.1 rebounds, and 2.1 blocks. His field goal percentage of .619 was among the best in the country. He was a first-team All-American and the Big Ten Conference's Most Outstanding Player. He was a finalist for two awards—the Wooden and the Naismith—which go to the country's top college player.

Michigan was the most exciting team in the nation. It was also one of the best. The Wolverines finished the regular season with 26 wins and just 4 losses. They were the fifth-ranked school in the polls. Heading back to the NCAA Tournament, they expected to cruise through to the final game.

That did not quite happen. Sure, Michigan cruised past Coastal Carolina in the first round. But in the next game, they fell behind UCLA, 55–33, at halftime. After a lecture from Coach Fisher, they came out for the second half and went on a 27–10 run. The highlights included three dunks by Webber, one of which shook the backboard for ten seconds. The game went into overtime and was tied, 84–84, with 9 seconds to go in overtime. Webber passed the ball to Jalen Rose, who soared toward the basket. Rose's shot banked off the rim, but teammate Jimmy King was there to tap it in. The Wolverines escaped with a win.

They went on to easy victories against George Washington University and Temple University. Now they were back in the Final Four. They faced Kentucky, which was led by star forward Jamal Mashburn. Once again, the game went into overtime. The Wolverines were ahead, 79–78, with just 4 seconds left. Michigan needed one more defensive stand. Kentucky guard Rodney Dent tried to pass the ball into Mashburn—but Webber slapped it back at Dent's face. Dent tried again, and this time, Webber tipped the ball and caught it.

The game ended. Michigan had won. The Fab Five would get another shot at the title.

The infamous game against North Carolina came on April 5, 1993. In the locker room before the game, Webber looked at teammate Rob Pelinka's championship ring. Pelinka earned the ring as a freshman in 1989, when Michigan won the NCAA tournament. At that time, Webber was just a high school sophomore.

Appearing on national TV before the game, Webber said that he had always dreamed of being in a national title game. "I never thought it would come to reality," he said. "Making it to two Final Fours and two championship games is something I never could fathom."

As exciting as the Fab Five were, North Carolina was quiet and steady. The Tar Heels played a slow team game, led by center Eric Montross. Carolina coach Dean Smith did not like flashy players. In fact, Smith was one of the few college coaches who did not recruit Webber out of high school.

The game was a close one early on. Webber crashed past Montross for a thunderous dunk. "Get used to that," he screamed at Montross. "I'm here all night." But Montross came back with a dunk of his own. At halftime, Carolina led, 42–36.

Webber remembered how badly the second half had gone in the title game a year before, so he came out for the second half full of energy. He was grabbing rebounds, blocking shots, and making key baskets. The exciting game went back and forth, with each team taking and then losing the lead. On a play with two minutes to go, Webber sneaked up behind Carolina's Donald Williams. He reached over Williams's head and tapped the ball away. He grabbed the loose ball and headed to the basket for a dunk.

And so it went. The Wolverines were down, 72–69, with

Although he played a great game, Chris Webber is still remembered for calling the timeout that ended the University of Michigan's hopes of winning the 1993 NCAA tournament.

just .48 left. Jalen Rose tried a three-pointer, which missed. Webber grabbed the rebound and rolled it in. Now Michigan was down by one.

Carolina got the ball back. Michigan quickly fouled. The Tar Heels' Pat Sullivan made the first shot, giving his team a two-point lead. But he missed the second. Webber grabbed the rebound and began heading downcourt. He appeared intent on making a basket to tie or even win the game. But when two Carolina defenders closed in on him, Webber felt trapped. He did not pass. He didn't shoot. Instead, he stopped dribbling and called the awful timeout that Michigan did not have. The game was lost.

It was a horrible way for a great game to end. Webber knew he had cost his team a chance at the title. He cried afterward and hugged his dad. Most people felt sorry for him. NBA star Isiah Thomas of the Detroit Pistons came to see him. Webber's old hero, Magic Johnson, suggested they work out together. Even President Bill Clinton called to offer support.

"It's funny," Webber said a few days later. "That timeout really helped my popularity. People saw a human side of me in a situation that caused me to weep."

Chapter 4

Two days after Michigan lost the 1993 NCAA title game, Chris Webber and his Wolverines teammates were greeted by thousands of fans at the University of Michigan's Crisler Arena. If the fans were angry at Webber, they sure did not show it. Instead, they gave him a standing ovation. And Webber returned the warm feelings. "It would be great to stand in front of all these people after winning a championship," he said.

That would mean staying in school. But as much as Webber loved it on the Ann Arbor campus, there were other issues to consider. The biggest was money. College athletes are not paid, beyond attending classes and living at school for free. Webber's family had little money, and he was tired of having to scrimp and save just to afford a weekend pizza. If he left school to join the National Basketball Association, he could earn millions of dollars.

He made up his mind one day during a visit to the university bookstore. He saw other students lined up to buy Wolverines jerseys carrying his name and the number four.

The school was making money from the sales, but Webber was getting none of it. That struck him as unfair.

So on May 5, 1993, he announced he would leave college early. He entered his name into the NBA draft of college players. There was no doubt he would be an early pick. But how early?

With the draft a month away, Webber and his dad, Mayce Webber, Jr., visited some of the teams that might select him. They went to Oakland, California, to visit with Golden State Warriors coach Don Nelson and his son, Donn, who was the team's top scout. During a training drill, the muscular Webber took off his shirt to cool down. The Nelsons were awed. "He looked like Hulk Hogan," said Donn Nelson.

The Warriors desperately wanted Webber. But Golden State had the third pick of the draft, behind the Orlando Magic and Philadelphia 76ers. There was not much chance he would still be around by then. Most people thought Golden State would have to settle for one of the draft's other fine prospects, such as Jamal Mashburn from Kentucky, Shawn Bradley from Brigham Young, or Anfernee "Penny" Hardaway from Memphis State.

Webber really wanted to go to the Magic. Nothing excited him more than the chance to play with Orlando's young superstar, Shaquille O'Neal.

The draft was held on June 30, 1993. The first pick was made by the Magic—and they chose Webber. He was thrilled. He high-fived one of his brothers. He kissed his mom, Doris, on the cheek.

But the joy did not last long. After the 76ers took Shawn Bradley, the Warriors took Penny Hardaway. Then a trade was made. The Magic sent Webber to Golden State in return for Hardaway and three future first-round draft picks.

Webber was disappointed, but ready to go to Golden State. He put on a Warriors baseball cap and posed with Coach

Chris Webber takes on Shaquille O'Neal of the Orlando Magic. In 1993, Webber was drafted by the Magic but quickly traded to the Golden State Warriors.

Nelson. Speaking to a crowd of forty-five hundred fans in Oakland, the coach said, "Our time is now. Chris has the best hands I've ever seen. This guy catches everything."

Webber quickly signed a fifteen-year, $74 million contract. That was an all-time high for a rookie. He worked out hard, dropping from 265 to 246 pounds. Then, just before the season opened, Webber came down with appendicitis. He needed surgery, and he missed the first two weeks of the season. Other bad breaks hit the Warriors. Tim Hardaway, the all-star guard, tore up his knee in practice. He missed the entire year. And star forward Chris Mullin ripped a finger ligament and had to sit out for twenty games.

When Webber recovered, Coach Nelson changed his position from power forward to center. Webber was unhappy. He had played forward throughout high school and college. But he vowed to give center a try.

It certainly seemed to work. Webber snared ten or more rebounds in his first three games. In his fourth game, against the Phoenix Suns, Webber made a highlight-film move. He raced down the floor on a fast break and caught a high pass. He faked out Phoenix defender Charles Barkley by spinning the ball around his waist. Then he brought the crowd to its feet by rising over Barkley for a massive dunk.

The great games continued. Against the Seattle SuperSonics, Webber pulled down 18 rebounds. Against the Los Angeles Clippers, he had his first triple-double: 22 points, 12 rebounds, and 12 assists.

Golden State's fans began to adore their hot rookie. And Webber wanted to give back to the community. He hosted a Christmas party in Oakland to feed 138 homeless people. His new charity—recalling his famous college blunder—was called Take Time Out.

By midseason, Webber and Orlando's Penny Hardaway

were the NBA's top rookies. Webber showed flashes of brilliance that grew more steady. He was the tall, strong inside force the Warriors had long needed. Some said he was the first good big man on Golden State since Hall of Fame center Nate Thurmond had been traded in 1974.

"He is the best thing that has happened to this franchise, and to me personally, in the last dozen years," said Coach Nelson. "He is doing things around the basket that have not been seen here in quite a while. The scary thing about Chris Webber is that he's going to get so much better."

Most admirable was Webber's work ethic. When he joined the NBA, for instance, he had no idea how to play with his back to the basket. But he worked day after day, staying late at practice. He asked coaches and other players to help him develop moves. By the end of his rookie season, he learned to play with his back facing the basket. He learned an assortment of what are called low-post moves.

He put those moves to full use in a February 1994 game against the Utah Jazz. Playing against superstar forward Karl Malone, Webber used a variety of spin moves and shoulder fakes to baffle the more experienced defender. He put up 27 points. Late in the game, with the score tied, Webber flew past Malone for a tomahawk dunk that caused the backboard to rattle. The play gave the Warriors the lead for good. Hometown fans responded with a standing ovation.

Webber also learned to take better care of himself away from the game. He made sure he got his sleep. And he gave up many of his favorite foods.

"I can't eat a lot of junk food," he said. "I love potato chips, I always used to eat barbecue chips and candy and drink pop. I learned that you can't do that because you won't have as much energy."

Webber was the youngest player among more than three

Webber worked hard to improve during his rookie season. His team improved as well, winning sixteen more games than it had the year before.

hundred in the NBA. But his playing did not show his youth. By season's end, his numbers were awesome. He became the first rookie ever to get more than 1,000 points, 500 rebounds, 250 assists, 150 blocks, and 75 steals. In fact, just three veterans had ever accomplished that feat—Kareem Abdul-Jabbar, Hakeem Olajuwon, and David Robinson. Webber was in great company.

Led by Webber, the Warriors improved to 50 wins, up from 34 the season before he arrived. Even with all their injuries, Golden State made the NBA playoffs. They were quickly knocked out in three games by Barkley's Phoenix Suns. Still, it had been a very successful season.

The writers and broadcasters who cover the NBA agreed. At season's end, they voted Webber the league's Rookie of the Year. He received fifty-three first-place votes to Hardaway's forty-seven. Webber was delighted.

But there were rumblings of problems. Webber and Coach Nelson had battled during the season. Both men, however, kept their fights quiet for the good of the team. Now it was all coming out. Webber told reporters that he did not like playing center. He complained that the coach had benched him too often late in close games. Meanwhile, Coach Nelson said that Webber had stopped improving his game as the season wore on.

"Coach told the guards that the reason we were losing was Chris Webber," said teammate Billy Owens. One week later, Owens was traded to the Miami Heat. That made Webber feel even worse.

The more rumors that came out, the more unhappy Webber became. He knew that pro basketball was a business, but he did not enjoy his job anymore. And his father had taught him never to keep a job he did not love.

After a while, Webber and his coach stopped talking to each other. And Webber decided to push the issue to the edge.

During his rookie year, Chris Webber had a falling out with Coach Don Nelson. As a result, Webber was eventually traded to the Washington Bullets.

His contract had a clause allowing him to end the deal and become a restricted free agent after his rookie season. It was a risk—he might have to settle for less money somewhere else—but he took it. Never again, he said, would he play for Nelson or Golden State. But even he did not know what would happen next.

Chapter 5

Chris Webber was back in Detroit when the 1994–95 National Basketball Association season opened. He refused to play for Coach Don Nelson and the Golden State Warriors, so he sat at home, watching other NBA teams play on television. He grew more and more depressed about basketball. Why couldn't it be as much fun as it had been in college?

"There's a part of me that felt like the sun set when I left Michigan," he said. "Part of me feels like I've already had a taste of heaven. We felt like the dorm we lived in was our penthouse. There was so much happiness in everything. To me, that was everything basketball should be."

And now, he thought, basketball was about fighting with his coach. It was about worrying over money. It was about fans calling him a spoiled brat for demanding a trade. Funny, Webber thought. Sometimes life can be better before your dreams come true.

Then, he got a break. Two weeks into the season, Webber got a phone call. He had been traded, he was told. He was going to the Washington Bullets in exchange for forward Tom

Gugliotta and three first-round draft picks. For the second time in his short career, Chris Webber was the key man in a blockbuster swap.

Webber was thrilled to get a fresh start on a new team. He quickly signed a one-year contract with Washington. And there was even better news. His old college buddy, Juwan Howard, had been drafted by the Bullets and had just signed a contract. The two great friends would be reunited.

The Bullets, however, were a terrible team. They had gone 24–58 the season before. Their fans had turned off to the team, which had gone through seven straight losing seasons. Other than newcomers Webber and Howard, they did not have much of a lineup.

But the reunited Fab Five duo brought back excitement. The Bullets sold twelve hundred new season tickets the day after Webber and Howard arrived. When they played their first game on November 19, 1994, the sellout hometown crowd gave them a standing ovation.

"More than anything, this brings excitement to the team and the city," said first-year Washington coach Jimmy Lynam.

After just one practice with their new teammates, Webber and Howard were a bit rusty. Still, Howard had 10 points and 11 rebounds. Webber had 9 points, 9 rebounds, and 4 blocked shots. The bottom line, however, was not good. The Bullets lost the game.

In fact, the team lost twenty-three of its next twenty-six games. Webber was the team leader, but the team behind him was not good at all. To be fair, the Bullets were a young team. Both Webber and Howard were just twenty-one years old. Their next-best player, Calbert Cheaney, was just twenty-three. Coach Lynam knew they would take their lumps. But someday, he predicted, they would grow into winners.

"Chris Webber and Juwan Howard are undoubtedly the

Moving along the baseline, Chris Webber keeps his eye on the basket. Webber joined the Washington Bullets two weeks into the 1994–95 season.

heart of this team," Lynam said. "I envision this powerful pair of young forwards bringing us great depth and exceptional athletic ability."

Just as the duo began to click, there was more bad news. On December 22, 1994, Webber returned to Oakland for his first game against his old team, the Warriors. He was loudly booed by the fans. Wanting to show them—and Coach Nelson—how well he could do, he played extra hard. He dived for a stray ball in the second quarter and landed with his arm under his body. He heard a pop and felt immediate pain. Something was wrong.

Webber had dislocated his shoulder. It was a serious injury. He missed the next nineteen games as he worked hard to heal his shoulder. He sat on the sidelines in street clothes and watched as his teammates kept losing.

"It's hard when you're losing to enjoy what you are doing," he said. "It just gets to you. I take this job very seriously."

Webber returned for the end of the season. It was already a lost year—the Bullets had won just 21 games—but he and Howard wanted to finish strong. Near the end, things began to click.

Their best game of the season came in March 1995 against the tough Los Angeles Lakers. The Bullets had lost three games in a row. Before the contest, Webber and Howard vowed to their teammates that the losing streak was about to stop. Whatever it took, they said, they would win.

The team came out on fire. Early on, Howard flicked a behind-the-back pass to Webber, who cut through the key and scooped the ball over the outstretched arms of Lakers center Vlade Divac. It was two points on a play that would make the highlight reel. Webber took the ball outside and hit three straight perimeter shots over Lakers forward Cedric Ceballos. And when Divac came out to help cover Webber, Webber blew past him for a rim-shaking dunk.

On December 22, 1994, Webber injured his shoulder playing against his former team, the Golden State Warriors. Webber would have to miss the next nineteen games.

By the end of the night, Webber had a season high 31 points, 13 rebounds, and 11 assists. It was the season's high point for the Bullets as well, who got a rare victory.

Webber finished his first season in Washington averaging 20.1 points per game. That would have placed him in the league's top twenty-five if he had played in enough games to qualify. He also led the Bullets in rebounding and steals. As poorly as the team played, there was hope for the future with Webber and Howard.

Chris Webber was growing up on the basketball court. Off the court, he was growing up as well.

Webber has always had an interest in history, especially the history of his people. In 1995, he began collecting historical documents signed by famous African Americans. His collection now includes items signed by Civil War-era patriot Frederick Douglass and twentieth-century civil rights leader Martin Luther King, Jr. He also reads and collects books on African-American history.

Webber was once asked the question of who in history he would most like to be.

"I would not be anyone in history," he said. "I like being me at this point. I have the ability to influence history. I may be the person to find a cure for cancer or improve race relations. It is important for each of us to be ourselves and do what we can to make the world better for the next generation."

Webber's oncourt play and offcourt behavior pleased the Bullets' management. Just before the 1995–96 season opened, the club signed him to a six-year, $58 million contract. Team owner Abe Pollin proudly predicted, "We are going to bring an NBA championship to Washington. And Chris Webber is going to lead the way."

Would this be the year that things went right for Chris Webber and the team? Unfortunately, no. During the preseason,

Webber again dislocated his shoulder. He spent another month on the disabled list. He returned to the lineup around Thanksgiving and began to play his way into shape.

On December 28, 1995, Webber had the best game of his career. The Bullets were playing the Golden State Warriors. Webber always got pumped up for games against his former club. Before the game, he and Warriors guard Latrell Sprewell—one of Webber's best friends—bet a dinner on who would score more points that night. That got Webber even more pumped up.

As the game started, Webber took the first shot. It was a three-pointer, a rare shot for a tall man like him. It swished right through the basket. In fact, Webber hit his first six shots of the game. Taking passes from Howard and point guard Brent Price, he was hitting shots from all over the floor. On one play, he took a hard foul from Warriors forward Joe Smith. Webber fell backward as the referee's hand went up to signal a foul against Smith. He took a shot as he landed on his back. The ball bounced off the backboard through the net for two points. Webber then converted the foul shot for a three-point play.

By game's end, Webber's statistics were terrific. He scored 40 points as the Bullets took an easy victory. Webber hit eighteen of twenty-five shots from the floor. He also grabbed 10 rebounds and added 11 assists. He won his friendly bet with Sprewell, who finished with 21 points.

"I was just in a zone tonight," he told reporters in the locker room afterward. "I can't take all the credit, though. This was a total team effort. It just feels good to get that win."

With Webber in the lineup, the Bullets won nine of fifteen games. The team was clicking. Webber averaged a team-high 23.7 points per game. He also led the club in rebounds and assists. It is very rare for a big man to lead a club in assists, but Webber's passing is outstanding.

Pleased with Chris Webber's performance, Washington signed him to a six-year, $58 million contract before the start of the 1995–96 season.

Disaster would strike again. Two nights after he single-handedly destroyed the Warriors, Webber led the Bullets against the tough New York Knicks. He played the whole game, and the Bullets scored an upset victory. But as the night went on, Webber's shoulder began aching again. The more he played, the more it ached.

The news was not good. Doctors said that Webber had strained his bad shoulder fighting for a rebound against Knicks center Patrick Ewing. They told him to rest it for a few weeks, hoping it would get better. But after a month, there was no improvement. Webber finally underwent surgery on February 1, 1996. Once again, he was through for the season.

There is no arguing that Chris Webber is a great basketball player. And there is no arguing that he has had his share of bad breaks. From the infamous timeout in the NCAA title game to the many injuries he has suffered as a pro, tough times seem to follow Webber.

"My back is always against the wall," he once said. "I feel like I've always done well when my back is against the wall. My mother keeps telling me that there's got to be good times ahead, to make up for the bad times I've had."

Perhaps the 1996–97 season would mark the end of the bad times. Chris Webber could only hope so.

Chapter 6

Chris Webber awoke at dawn on April 20, 1997. That was unusual for him. Usually, when his team had a night game coming up, Webber liked to sleep until 10 A.M.

But this day was different. On this day, Webber's Washington Bullets would play their most important game of the season. For Webber, it was his most important game since he had left the University of Michigan four years earlier.

It was the final day of the NBA regular season. The Bullets were tied with the Cleveland Cavaliers in a battle for the last Eastern Conference playoff spot. The two teams were to play that night. The winner would face the Chicago Bulls in the playoffs. The loser would go home empty-handed.

So Webber sat in bed at dawn. He thought back to that fateful NCAA championship game in 1993. He remembered calling the timeout that helped cost his team the game.

"I thought about that feeling you get when you lose," he said. "It's a terrible feeling. Everything inside is just so empty. I didn't want to have that again. I wanted to do anything I could so I wouldn't have to feel it again."

He took an early taxi to Cleveland's Gund Arena. He focused on his job that night—outproducing Cleveland forwards Danny Ferry and Chris Mills. As his teammates showed up in the locker room, Webber gave each a pep talk. "Let's show some emotion," he shouted at center Gheorghe Muresan.

When the game began, Webber took charge. He was a rebounding demon, grabbing 17 missed shots. That was more than Cleveland's two top rebounders combined. With the game tied, 72–72, with four minutes left, Webber breezed by Cavaliers center Tyrone Hill for a lay-up. On the next possession, he grabbed a rebound and fed the ball to teammate Calbert Cheaney for a dunk. The game was all but over.

The Bullets won, 85–81. Webber had a great night. He finished with 23 points and 4 assists. Most important, he helped put his team in the playoffs. In crunch time, the guy with a reputation for choking under pressure really came through.

"How much did I want this?" Webber asked after the game. "I cried because we won, and this isn't even the championship or anything. But after two years of injuries, after coming into Washington and not living up to expectations, this really meant something."

Webber's entire season meant quite a bit. He stayed healthy for the first time since his rookie season, and the results showed. He led his team by averaging 20.1 points, 10.3 rebounds, and 1.9 blocks per game. For the first time, he was selected to play in the NBA All-Star Game. The Bullets won nineteen of their final twenty-six games to get into the playoffs. And Webber was the NBA's Player of the Week for the season's final week, when he led the team to four straight wins.

What was the difference in his play and the team's? Webber said it was maturity.

"Any type of adversity we have faced, we have all come closer," he said. "I think we all grow and we experience different

During the 1996–97 season, Chris Webber helped lead the Bullets to the playoffs for the first time since 1988.

problems. That's everyone—from the mailman to my father, who was an auto worker. We all have to learn to deal with the problems that face us."

The Bullets' reward for making the playoffs was no great prize. The team got to face the Chicago Bulls, once again the league's top team. No one was surprised when the Bulls knocked out Washington in three straight games. What was surprising was how closely the Bullets played Michael Jordan and company. Each game was dead even until the final minutes. So even as Washington was knocked out quickly, there was cause to feel good about the team.

"There is no question that they could have beaten a lot of teams," said Bulls star Scottie Pippen. "Chris Webber and Juwan Howard and [point guard] Rod Strickland give them a lot to build on. As that team grows up, they'll be trouble for everyone."

Off the court, Chris Webber was growing up as well. He tried his hand at acting, appearing in an episode of the television show *New York Undercover* and the movie *Space Jam*. He also tried singing with two rap groups—Jodeci and Total. He briefly dated actress Nia Long but found that playing in the NBA kept him from having enough time to develop a steady relationship.

"There is so little free time during the season," he said. "I usually eat a good meal after practice and then go to sleep. If it's a game night, I will read a book, phone home, watch the other games on television or play video games."

Webber also tries to keep a low profile because he believes that some people are out to make star athletes look bad. In January 1998, he was arrested in Maryland while driving to a morning practice. He was charged with driving under the influence of marijuana and assaulting a police officer. Webber denied the charges. He said he was targeted only because of his fame. He was eventually cleared on all charges.

In truth, Webber is a professional athlete with both a conscience and a big heart. He is involved with charities that feed the hungry and house the poor. In 1998, he donated twenty-five thousand dollars to a scholarship fund for college science students. And unlike many athletes who endorse products, Webber took a stand on the high price of sneakers. When Nike refused his request to price his signature shoes so that inner-city kids could afford them, Webber ended his contract with Nike. Instead, he signed a deal with the Fila shoe company. Part of the contract ensures that his sneakers sell for less than one hundred dollars a pair.

After finishing strong in 1996–97, Webber could not wait for the next season to begin. There was much to be excited about. On a small note, the team changed its name, from the Bullets to the Washington Wizards. It was not a big deal, but Webber liked the change, especially when he saw the new blue-and-copper-colored uniforms. The Wizards also moved into a new home, the modern MCI Arena in downtown Washington, D.C.

With Webber, Howard, and Strickland as a nucleus, the Wizards were expected to be an outstanding team in 1997–98. How good? Well, New York Knicks coach Jeff Van Gundy said at season's start, "I think that outside of Chicago, obviously, Washington has as much talent as any team in the East."

Webber and his teammates thought they could contend for a division title. But it did not happen. On some nights, the Wizards played great. On others, they were awful. For example, on one Saturday, they lost to a bad Dallas Mavericks club by 28 points. The next afternoon, they beat the Pacific Division-leading Los Angeles Lakers. No one could figure out why they were so inconsistent.

The team's chances were hurt when seven-foot, seven-inch center Gheorghe Muresan went down for the year with an

For the start of the 1997–98 season, Washington's basketball team was renamed the Wizards. Webber liked the change and the team's new blue-and-copper uniforms.

injury. But even without Muresan, the Wizards should have played better.

"I wish I could give you the answers," Webber said toward the end of the season. "But I don't know what they are. Is it concentration? Is it experience? Is it injuries? It's probably a combination."

Once again, the Wizards' playoff chances came down to the season's final day. This time, however, they fell one game short. They won 42 games—one less than the New Jersey Nets. The Nets grabbed the final playoff spot. The Wizards went home disappointed.

On a personal level, he did enjoy one of his finest seasons. He averaged 21.9 points per game, tenth best in the entire NBA. He also ranked among league leaders in blocks and minutes played.

The 1997–98 season was Webber's fifth in pro basketball. Still, at the season's end, he was just twenty-five years old. By his own reckoning, he had another ten years left as a player. And he did not plan to quit the job any time soon.

"The best part of playing in the NBA is that it's not a job, it's an experience," Webber said. "Generally, there is something about a job that is not appealing. The hours are not good. Or the job is boring. Or you don't have an opportunity to use your skills. In the NBA, you are rewarded for developing and disciplining your skills. Playing the game is anything but boring."

Disappointed with the way the season turned out, the Wizards decided that a change was in order. Webber was traded to the Sacramento Kings for shooting guard Mitch Richmond and power forward Otis Thorpe. Now Webber would try to help rebuild one of the worst teams in the NBA.

Webber's top goal, he said, is to win an NBA championship. Certainly the Kings have a long way to go. But he remembers the 1993 NCAA title game, and then remembers how close he

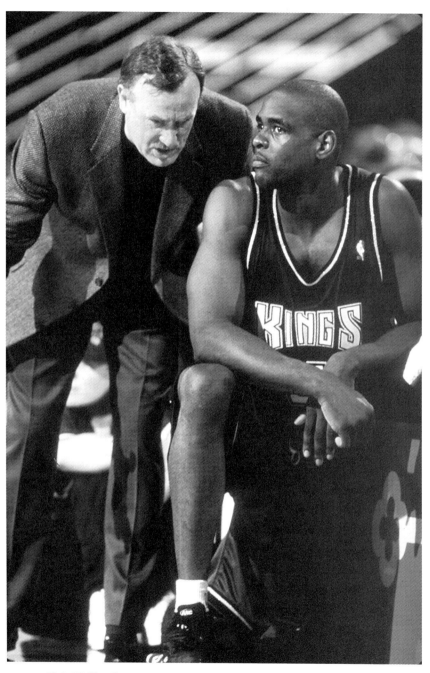
Chris Webber listens to the instructions of Sacramento Kings coach Rick Adelman. Webber was traded to the Kings prior to the 1999 season.

During his first five seasons in the NBA, Chris Webber averaged more than 20 points and 9 rebounds per game. The Kings hope that Webber can be even better, and lead the franchise to an NBA title.

came to winning it all once before. Losing that game at the end was frustrating. He wants another chance at the big one.

His other goal is to be remembered at the end of his career as one of the best players ever. It is too early to judge whether he will make it. Injuries cut his playing time twice in his first five seasons. And Webber has yet to play for a winner. Most great players—from Larry Bird to Magic Johnson to Michael Jordan—are remembered for producing victories and not just points or rebounds.

In his first season in Sacramento, Webber wasted no time in waking up the Kings. The posted its highest winning percentage (.540) in seventeen seasons and landed in the NBA playoffs for only the second time in the 1990s.

With solid center Vlade Divac and sensational rookie Jason Williams added to the mix, the Kings ran a high-flying end-to-end offense. They wound up as the highest-scoring team in the

NBA. Webber averaged 20.1 points and a league-leading 13.0 rebounds per game.

"I'm definitely enjoying myself here in Sacramento," Webber said early in 1999. "It's funny what a difference a year can make. I want to believe this is where I'll play for the rest of my career."

The young and hungry Kings were not just content making the playoffs. Sacramento went on the road and beat the Utah Jazz in Game 2 of their first-round playoff series. Webber scored, rebounded, dished, and even hit two clutch shots down the stretch. He showed fans why he was a dark horse MVP candidate.

Then in Game 3, the Kings sent the defending Western Conference champs to the brink of elimination. The Kings beat the Jazz in a thrilling overtime game. The Jazz, however, came back to win the next two games, sending Webber and his teammates home.

Through his first six seasons, Chris Webber averaged about 20 points and 10 rebounds per game. Those are outstanding numbers. There is a drive and dedication that suggest he will produce in the NBA for years to come. If the Kings develop into a better team, he may earn his place among the all-time stars of the game.

It would be a great reward for a man who is still remembered for the classy way he handled his greatest moment of failure.

Career Statistics

College

YEAR	TEAM	GP	FG%	REB	PTS	AVG
1991–92	Michigan	34	.556	340	528	15.5
1992–93	Michigan	36	.619	362	690	19.2
Totals		70	.589	702	1,218	17.4

NBA

YEAR	TEAM	GP	FG%	REB	AST	STL	BLK	PTS	AVG
1993–94	Golden State	76	.552	694	272	93	164	1,333	17.5
1994–95	Washington	54	.495	518	256	83	85	1,085	20.1
1995–96	Washington	15	.543	114	75	27	9	356	23.7
1996–97	Washington	72	.518	743	331	122	137	1,445	20.1
1997–98	Washington	71	.482	674	273	111	124	1,555	21.9
1998–99	Sacramento	42	.486	545	173	60	89	839	20.0
Totals		330	.508	3,288	1,380	496	608	6,613	20.0

GP=Games Played **AST**=Assists **PTS**=Points scored
FG%=Field Goal Percentage **STL**=Steals **AVG**=Points per game
REB=Rebounds **BLK**=Blocks

Where to Write Chris Webber:

Mr. Chris Webber
c/o Sacramento Kings
One Sports Parkway
Sacramento, CA 95834

On the Internet at:

http://www.nba.com/playerfile/chris_webber.html
http://www.nba.com/Kings

Index

A
Abdul-Jabbar, Kareem, 40
Ali, Muhammad, 25, 26
Amateur Athletic Union (AAU), 17
Auburn University, 22

B
Barkley, Charles, 22, 37, 40
Bird, Larry, 11, 28, 59
Bradley, Shawn, 35
Brigham Young University, 35

C
Ceballos, Cedric, 45
Cheaney, Calbert, 43, 52
Chicago Bulls, 51, 54
Cleveland Cavaliers, 51, 52
Clinton, President Bill, 33
Coastal Carolina University, 30
Coleman, Derrick, 17

D
Dallas Mavericks, 55
Dent, Rodney, 30
Detroit Country Day School, 17, 19–20
Detroit Pistons, 33
Divac, Vlade, 45, 59
Douglass, Frederick, 47
Drexler, Clyde, 28
Duke University, 26

E
East Tennessee University, 24
Ewing, Patrick, 50

F
Fab Five, 7, 20, 24, 25–26, 28, 31, 43
Ferry, Danny, 52
Fisher, Steve, 8, 9, 20, 30

G
George Washington University, 30
Golden State Warriors, 9, 35, 37–38, 40–41, 42, 48
Gugliotta, Tom, 42–43
Gund Arena, 52

H
Hardaway, Anfernee "Penny," 35, 37
Hardaway, Tim, 37
Hervey, Curtis, 16–17
Hill, Tyrone, 52
Hogan, Hulk, 35
Howard, Juwan, 20, 24, 43, 45, 54, 55

I
Indiana University, 28

J
Jackson, Ray, 20, 28
Jent, Chris, 24
Johnson, Magic, 11, 13, 28, 33, 59
Jordan, Michael, 11, 22, 28, 54, 59

K
King, Bernard, 13
King, Jimmy, 20, 30
King, Jr., Martin Luther, 47
Knight, Bobby, 28
Krzyzewski, Mike, 26

L
Laettner, Christian, 26
Long, Nia, 54
Los Angeles Clippers, 37
Los Angeles Lakers, 45, 55
Lynam, Jimmy, 43, 45

M
Malone, Karl, 38
Mashburn, Jamal, 30, 35
Memphis State University, 35
Miami Heat, 40
Michigan State University, 28
Mills, Chris, 52

Montross, Eric, 31
Mullin, Chris, 37
Muresan, Gheorghe, 52, 55, 57

N

Naismith Award, 30
NBA All-Star Game (1997), 52
NBA Rookie of the Year Award, 40
NCAA Championship Game, (1992), 26
NCAA Championship Game, (1993), 8–9, 11, 31, 33, 34
Nelson, Don, 11, 35, 37, 38, 40–41, 42, 45
Nelson, Donn, 35
New Jersey Nets, 57
New York Knicks, 50, 55
New York Undercover, 54

O

Ohio State University, 24
Olajuwon, Hakeem, 40
O'Neal, Shaquille, 35
Orlando Magic, 35
Owens, Billy, 40

P

Parade magazine, 20
Pelinka, Rob, 26, 31
Philadelphia 76ers, 35
Phoenix Suns, 37, 40
Pippen, Scottie, 54
Pollin, Abe, 47
Price, Brent, 48

R

Richmond, Mitch, 57
Robinson, David, 40
Rose, Jalen, 15, 16–17, 20, 24, 30, 33

S

Sacramento Kings, 57, 59–60
Seattle SuperSonics, 37

Smith, Dean, 31
Smith, Joe, 48
Space Jam, 54
Sprewell, Latrell, 48
Strickland, Rod, 54, 55
Sullivan, Pat, 33

T

Temple University, 24, 30
Thomas, Isiah, 33
Thorpe, Otis, 57
Thurmond, Nate, 38

U

United States Olympic Basketball Team, 28
University of California Los Angeles (UCLA), 30
University of Cincinnati, 25
University of Detroit Mercy, 22
University of Kentucky, 30, 35
University of Michigan, 7–9, 20, 22, 24, 25–26, 28, 30–31, 33, 34, 51
University of North Carolina, 8–9, 11, 22, 31, 33
University of Oklahoma, 24
Utah Jazz, 38, 60

V

Van Gundy, Jeff, 55

W

Washington Bullets, 42–43, 45, 47–48, 50, 51–52, 53, 54
Washington Wizards, 54, 57
Webber, Doris, 11
Webber, Mayce, Jr., 11, 15, 35
Williams, Donald, 31
Williams, Jason, 59
Willis, Kevin, 17
Wooden Award, 30